COFFEE-STAINED REFLECTIONS

BY STACY HINOJOS

OCYD Publishing

Published by OCYD Publishing
https://www.thesewords.blog/

ISBN: 979-8-9912807-3-0

To those who support dreams
and the dream makers.

Thank you.

Preface

Coffee-Stained Reflections was born from my need to establish a daily writing habit. The challenge was to finish at least one piece that I felt was publishable each and every day over the last year. Not only did it force me to maintain a decent work ethic, but it also gave me the opportunity to go through the mountains of incomplete pieces that had been gathering dust for far too long.

Coffee-Stained Reflections contains a variety of poetic pieces and meandering thoughts, touching on a multitude of themes. I hope you find something enjoyable within these pages.

In gratitude,
Stacy

Table of Contents

An Introduction

It's early morning, half past four, the birds aren't even singing yet, and I am awake. I make my way down the dark staircase and shuffle to the kitchen. I am in need of a large mug full of a dark roast, mana for my soul.

Despite me longing for the warmth and comfort of my bed, I cannot sleep, or quiet the voices in my head. Instead, I'll curl up in the corner of the couch, journal and pen in hand, and write.

I sip on my coffee, breathing it in while pondering what words I'll pluck out of the air to begin weaving a poetic tale about those voices in my head.

I lean over to set my mug of coffee down on a small table, which is laden with piles of notebooks and stacks of journals. However, I am misguided in the placement of my mug, and half of the contents splash over the lip.

The muddy river of caffeine snakes towards an old composition book, dated 2016, not so old memories. Reflections now the color of coffee and cream.

January

1
Instead of mapping out Resolutions,
we should be planning Revolutions.

2
Cold, grey January,
the first of the winter snow has nearly gone.
No sun in the sky,
only the last of the geese heading south.

3
heal in the sunshine!
    heal in the rain!
        heal out loud!

    do not try to heal
        alone and
            in silence.

4
It is difficult to express how you feel
when you're holding your tongue
afraid of what words might tumble out.

5
I can still remember the first time you said my name.

It felt like home.

6 *(In remembrance of M.L.McG.)*
Oh, how I wish I could hear an Eastern Screech Owl.
His song would pull at my heart,
yet it would feel like a hug.

7
Death,
I am afraid,
Is the only thing we have in common.

8
you are beautiful when
you are being honest

9 *(In remembrance of President Jimmy Carter.)*
People say you shouldn't meet your heroes,
because you'll be disappointed by every single one.

But I would have taken my chances with Jimmy Carter.

10
Sitting here with a mountain of notebooks,
wondering if the words inside actually mean anything.

11
I'm only asking you to please

please

love me more than I love myself.

12
How can I let go
When I'm made to feel guilty
About something I had
No control over.

13
Do not place unachievable expectations onto me.

Especially if you wouldn't hold yourself to the same expectations.

14
She looked me right in the eye and said…

"Yes, that should be you in the box."

15
Why did you jump in front of me,
if you were just going to slow me down?

16
life goes on whether I'm living
or not

17
I have lived most of my life half asleep.
I hadn't realized until you swept me off my feet.

18
Stop.
Shh.
Listen.
Listen with your eyes wide open.

19 *(The night TikTok went black.)*
I spent the evening doom scrolling,
Until the app went black.
Suddenly, I feel so disconnected.

20
I never thought I would see someone
give the Sieg Heil at the podium
of the Presidential inauguration.

They are no long hiding.

21
I sometimes hate how much I love you.
How easily I forgive the things you say or do.

22
I am sitting here,
waiting for the other shoe to drop.
Watching for the first lace to break.

23
the old black and white photo
in the faded Bakelite frame
keeping the dust off the
smiling faces of two children
sitting on the moon

24 *(Dedicated to Bishop Mariann Edgar Budde.)*
She stepped up to that pulpit said what countless others should have said but feared too.

Not only was she brave to say them, but she spoke those words as she stared into his eyes.

25
I have run out of words for…
Encouragement
Love
Sympathy
Empathy
and Grace…
because you keep throwing them back in my face.

26
We often learn the hardest lessons when others ignore our hurt.

27
Look at the empty cup you hold in your hand.
Now try to drink from it.

28 *(Is it really procrastination if I'm reading?)*
I should be writing a book.
I could be writing a book.
I would be writing a book,
But I found a book on the shelf to read!

29
I sometimes wonder how I got this far,
and what the point could be.
Because I'm exhausted,
but in the most poetic way.

30
The stars look down at me,
Slumbering away,
Even though I'm nothing special.

31 *(Co-written between giggle snorts with JMB when I needed a laugh.)*
I found Jesus at the bottom of a Cracker Jack Box,
and he sang to me while he tapped danced.
He is more talented than I initially thought.

February

1
Do you feel that?
That's the signal.
The warning that our borrowed time is coming to an end.

2
I stumble...
Searching for what I long to say...
Fumbling words along the way...

3
you used me up
   then threw me away
      once I had nothing more to offer

discarded like a
   used paper plate
      with a hot dog and ketchup stain

4
I want to breathe you in,
like I did when we first kissed.

5
Cut it off…
Throw it out…
Let it go…
Burn the ties that bind.

6
Over a thousand moons,
Prophecies have been
Woven into beautiful tapestries.

7
She fell in awe at the
wonders life brings,
while watching meteors
whiz past in canvas
of the heavens.

8 *(An ode to migraines.)*
She woke with sleepy giants in her head,
stumbling and bumbling,
crashing into the sides of her brain.

9
The only thing between me and the heavens,
was the cold night sky.

10
There are days when I feel everything,
and days when I feel nothing at all.

11
I am a reluctant student of life.
The lessons are hard,
and the dog ate my homework.

12
I am not enough.
Yet I am too much.

13
I longed for a new perspective
so...
I sat on the other end of the couch.

14
hearts flutter red and pink
cupid's arrows lost
replaced with boomerangs.

15
When love triumphs,
we are healed.
We pass the love and healing forward,
like ripples on water.

16
The mountain seemed larger today than it was yesterday.
Last week it was merely a mole hill.

17 *(The eve of the anniversary of my cancer diagnosis.)*
Tomorrow is my personal D-Day.
Which is only funny because I was born on the anniversary of D-Day.
But it really isn't funny.

18
Today marks the sixth anniversary of hearing…

"I'm so sorry. You have lymphoma."

Going into a tailspin wondering if you'll be...
fighting the same demon that killed your mother.

19
my brain feels as f u z z y
as a licked lollipop
dropped onto a shag carpet

20
My brain feels like a beehive,
it's all a buzz.

21
My brain feels like a bouncy ball
a child bounced into a muddy puddle.

22
This crown of grey I wear upon my head has been earned.
It's an honor, and I wear it proudly.

23
I love you now,
I loved you then,
I'll love you on my dying bed.

24
Don't allow your heart to grow cold.
Don't allow the anger to take hold.

25
With all the mistakes I've made,
God willing, you still love me in the morning.

26
You sit across from me,
Waiting for an apology,
But I'm not sure what for.

27
Is a story ever done,
Is it ever fully told?

28
A man told me that I had disappointed him today.
Good.

March

1
Poetry is like architecture,
but with words that flow,
and a rhythm that sticks.

2
Where do your ghosts go in the daytime,
when the sun shines on your face?

3
I hate you
 but I hate
  myself more
   for loving you
    in the first place.

4
The world is full of brokenness, cruelty, darkness, fear.
But it can be full of joy, beauty, love, peace.
We need to heal what is broken in ourselves, to heal the world.

5
poetry is written
so hearts can sing!

6 *(To my mom on her birthday.)*
You were born on this day sixty-nine years ago.
You had a laugh that could be heard across a grocery store,
and a smile that lit up a room.
I choose today to be thankful for lessons of love learned.

7
These moments we hold in our hands,
memories of everything good,
and everything bad.
Dreams realized,
and the dreams that have passed.
Tears which have fallen,
and love had.
These are mementos of a life lived.

8
it's early morning
4 o' clock
the owls are calling
whoooooo are they calling for?

9
why do we feel we need to give ourselves permission to feel
to express our emotions and share them with the world?

10
There are invisible wounds,
between me and you.
We try our best to ignore them,
instead of trying our best to heal them.

11
Writing offers me
a safe place to...
strengthen my voice
and heal the pain.

12
Inspiration strikes
at the most
i n c o n v e n i e n t
moments.
I walk
a r o u n d
repeating the words
over and over and
o v e r
like a mantra
until I find a pen.

13
I need to apologize to myself for not believing in the **strength** of my own voice.

14
not every day feels poetic

15
The Ides of March are here again
full of misfortune and doom.
What hides around the corner?
What whispers do you hear?
And for whom?

16
I don't remember requesting to live a life like this.
Perpetually worried if I matter at all.

17
They are wrapping their skeletons in angry red flags
and stuffing them into glass closets.
Everything in plain sight.

18
When the truth gets wrapped around your neck,

I hope you choke to death.

19
She swept through our lives like a landslide,
Washing away everything that was good in all of us,
Leaving only mud behind.

20
One day you are holding onto something rare and beautiful,
and the next day it all shatters into ribbons of sliver,
and flecks of gold.

21
If a heart doesn't hurt, has it known love?
If a bird doesn't sing,
how else would you know it has a song?

22
His love was aspartame sweet
and heavy like a humid summer day.

23
the weight of your love
pulled me beneath the surface
grey and cold

24
My heart hangs heavy like the branches
of an old willow tree.

The winds try to sway me,
but heavy hearts hang low.

25 *(To J.M.J.F on his birthday.)*
I miss the happy smiley boy who used to hide

s
n
a
i
l
s

in the pocket of his overalls.

26
She sits in her own bubble,
trying to block out the sounds of the living.
Holding her breath,
longing for something better.

27
the road is long
longer than my dreams
running down through
the evergreens

28
Open your eyes
The world awaits
Spread your wings
Fly, fly, fly away

29
Her love wore thin.
His lies he rarely hid.
Trust flaked away,
Until nothing remained.

30
If I had blinked
I would have missed her
Small wispy cloud above
An angel

31
The keeper of all my secrets,
and they do not judge,
will always be a journal,
and my favorite pen.

April

1
Once again, I will be appearing in the role of the fool,
a target for those who long to be cruel.

2
I'm empty and aching,
and I'm going to keep pretending,
that I don't know why.

3
I'm up on stage looking over the heads of the audience.
My nerves kicked in and I glanced down
at their polite smiles
or maybe their frowns of impatience at waiting
to hear their favorite poet or poem.

I put on my reading glasses and the crowd blurs.
Pretty vibrant smudges
as if I've just stepped much too closely
to an impressionist painting
and I'm trying to find meaning in the splotches.

4
Am I able to pretend long enough,
fool myself into believing,
that I deserve good things,
because I'm a better person than I used to be?

5

Some people work really hard to change,
even when they fall,
they pick up the pieces,
and try again.
While others work really hard at not even trying.

6

longing for summer days
sun-kissed faces
skin shining like sweet tea

7

Did I find you,
or did you find me?

In either case,
we were found,
finally seen.

8

Finding the things your soul longs for,
Should take you a lifetime,
As you continually change and grow.

9

When tomorrow doesn't come,
Hopefully you are at peace,
Slumbering in your bed,
That's full of thorns.

10
No one needs lessons on how to write poetry.
You only need to learn to be comfortable
with the words you wrote on the page.

11
I sit on my crying chair,
On my crying chair I did sit.
I let those tears fall and fall,
'til flowers grew at my feet.

12
I wonder why they still hurt me,
The words that have grown cold.
I don't try to warm them,
I thought I had swallowed them whole.

13 *(To my dad on his birthday.)*
unending love
a sacred pact
to love selflessly
and forever

14
Come along with me,
To release the unseen,
Pain ingrained,
Truth that burns,
Old words that still sting.

15
Fragile
Forgotten souls
That sprint past you
As you walk through the door.

16
Sometimes these moments still seem too good to be true.
Other times they feel like nightmares that run on a loop.

17
all their pain
was filtered
through the rain

18
He looked up at me,
as if I were a ghost.
It was like he forgot,
we lived in the same house.

19
This life is so fleeting.
This opportunity to breathe,
and be something,
do something,
stand up for something,
create something,

It is a lump of sugar,
At the bottom of your cup,
Before you start to pour.

20
I have a dream,
A far-fetched dream,
That our country
Will eventually unite
For the good of the country
And not the good of a few.

I did say it was far-fetched.

21
Pieces of me were scattered,
Thrown to the wind.
But you knew that,
You were the one throwing them.

22
I have found myself just north of "ok."
Down the block from "fine."
Across the corner from "eh."
South of "it will get better."

23
I can't heal
Hearing your
Voice in my head

It is an earworm
A recorded loop
Of constant doubt

24
The pile of notebooks I have
Scattered around the house,
Full of words plucked from the air,
Or whispered in my ears,
Is absurd.

And none of those words will come alive,
Until they are read.

25
The music in her heart,
A forgotten melody passed on to her from long ago,
Coursed through her body,
Like blood through her veins.

26
He stood back to watch her live.

It sometimes scared him,
the way she moved fearlessly,
through a world that didn't know how to love her.

27
The clarity I sought
Couldn't be found.
Not among the stars,
Nor dancing with the moon.

28

I don't want to hate you
But damn
You make it easy

29

Loyal and fierce,
Leading with her heart,
She slayed the dragons
Others were unwilling to face.

30

It's ok to say "no,"
even to yourself.

May

1
I ran out of minutes with you,
and my heart will be forever broken.

2
it would be so easy
to let you slip away
like night turning into day.

3
Reflections of who I was,
And where I've been,
Shattered mirrors of expectations
And lies I told myself.

4
hearts beat
whether they are broken or whole
a living rhythm
of movement
of breathing
of living

5
Wine glass sitting on the bar,
Half full,
Untouched,
Unwanted.
We've all been that glass of wine.

6
I thought I was aiming for heaven,
But it appears I stumbled right
Into the midst of hell.

7 *(A poetry prompt asking what loneliness tastes like.)*
Loneliness tastes like Neapolitan ice cream.
Sometimes loneliness tastes like vanilla,
plain and perhaps a little boring yet nourishing to the soul.
Sometimes loneliness tastes like chocolate,
rich and comforting yet a little naughty.
Sometimes loneliness tastes like strawberry,
fresh and sassy yet a little fun.
But sometimes, you have all three flavors in your bowl,
and loneliness is sheer perfection.

8
they were there,
inside me,
growing.
a little piece of you,
a little piece of me.
and they were gone in a whisper,
before they could be named.

9
Oh, how I need a drink.
The glass up to my lips,
sipping until all my memories
of you have been drowned
with the bottom of the bottle.

10
There is strength in pain,
Happiness in tears.
Anger in love,
Sadness to the breeze.

11
Breathing *should* be the easiest thing in the world.
It should be as automatic
as the sun rising in the east,
and setting in the west.

12
Tell me, friend,
what does your soul struggle with?

13
come to me
long-lost dreams of mine
let me dust off the hope
I once had

14
She said, "Time heals all wounds."

"No," I said.
"Time lessens the blow.
Time lessens the pain.
The wounds still exist,
the proof is the scar."

15

Her auburn hair blowing in the wind,
The summer sun making her glow.
She laughed as she danced,
And spun around in the sand.
Waves lapping at her legs and feet.
This was the most alive she'd ever been.

16

I long to crawl into my cozy bed,
And curse the world away.

17

I know that someday I'll get the answers I'm longing for.
I'll try not to be disappointed.

18

writing rhymes and
pondering paradigms
of modern times
while mimes spend dimes
on yellow limes
which should be a crime

19

By the time the sun sets,
she'll be on her way.
As she sits at the four-way stop,
she'll turn over the options in her head.
Which route will she take?

20
I lie awake
It's 12 a.m.
I'm writing rhymes
In my head
Wondering if I'll
Remember them
In the morning.

21
And we'll dance on the graves
Of the naughty men.

22
I am a ghost,
in my own life.
Melancholy.
Alone.
Unseen.
Yet I still breathe,
and my heart still beats.

23
We all have shadows that follow us around,
and sometimes we give them names.
Mine is grief.

24
The wine has made me misty
with thoughts of you.

25
I love the idea of things that…
Make my heart sing.
Make my soul glow.

26
Shouting out into the night about
    torn hearts
    love grown cold
    battles lost
    tarnished rings of gold.

Waiting for an answer
    in the silence
    that echoes back
    destroying what little bit was left.

27
This is how our silent wounds weep
in the darkness as pain festers
hearts drowning from shed tears.

28
Be curious about who you are.
Learn to like yourself, especially during the bad days.

29
Memories,
Both good and bad,
Can be floated away
By waves of tears.

30
my skin and bones are tired
and my brain feels like a soufflé
teetering on deflation

31
If everything is a dream away,
why am I still lying here in the dark
unable to fall asleep?

June

1
You convince yourself that what you…
saw…
heard…
felt…
Was all in your head.
But it wasn't.

2
I loved you once, that is true.
But I didn't understand, at that naïve age,
what love truly was, and the harm false love could do.

3
I thought loving you would be a privilege,
but it was a nightmare,
that played out during the day.

4
If there was a way I could go about my day
Without my mind drifting back to summer play
Maybe
Just maybe
I'd get over you.

5
She shimmered when she was happy,
And when she was in love, too.

It reminded him of the Californian sands.

6 *(It's my birthday!)*
I am a child born among the Big Bull Falls,
But raised along the shores of Gitchee Gumee,
The cold, clear waters of the bay christened Chequamegon.

I am a child raised where the white pines once reigned,
Where the noise of the sawmills drowned out the noise of men,
Shouting "timber," while hoisting cumbersome axes over their heads.

I am a child of music sung under a canvas of blue and silver,
Stars and moon shining down on Ashwabay,
Where stories are spun against a backdrop of old photographs.

I am a child of holding words that sting,
while writing words that heal what was broken,
creating the best version of me.

7
I stood under black clouds
hanging in an even blacker sky
the thunder rolled
lightning raced across the sky
the clouds burst forth
healing rains raced to my parched soul
washing away the sins from my body
and I was reborn

8
I don't want to be broken pieces scattered across the floor.
Splinters that dance in the sunlight waiting to be stepped on.
Hiding from the broom, hiding from the vacuum.

9 *(To my grandma on her birthday.)*
A grandmother's love was shown by…
playing games for hours
reading books on the deck
watching Lawrence Welk while eating potato chips in bed
making us feel safe
saying she was proud
singing how diamonds were a girl's best friend as she sewed
listening without judgment
laughing till our bodies ached
always being there when we needed help or advice.

10
He said…
Say a prayer for me.
I said…
I don't pray for the devil.

11
when you're looking
for solid ground
to wander on,
don't look down,
look forward.

12
You were my next chapter, another new verse.

13
They were just another face I knew...
gone way too soon.

14
Life is like a glass of lemonade.
With the bitter comes the sweet.

15
When my heart breaks
where do the pieces fall?
In your hand,
or mine?

16
I doubt each breath I take
While I watch the hands
Of a clock slowly make its way
Around his own face.

17
You extended your hand to help pull me out
from the depths of my own misery.
But you weren't strong enough to hold on.

18
I do not fear the dark,
As I bring the light.
I carry it
Wherever I go.

19
I hope each time my heart beats
You can feel it beat in sync with your own.

20
Deep breaths
1…2…3…

Heavy sighs
1…2…3…

If I stop focusing
1…2…3…

I will start to cry.

21
I can't keep picking up the pieces…

Trying to live each day…
Worn down and exhausted…

Burned by too many flames.

22
In those moments,
Sitting on the kitchen floor,
Being honest with you,
Being honest with myself,
Answering questions,
About what comes next,
Was a privilege.

23
She is as sharp and fragile as an icicle,
And about as transparent.

24
"You're talking in riddles," he accuses.

"No, I'm singing in rhyme
because if I shoot from the hip
you run and hide."

25
I often wish the broken parts of me would fall off
and float away on the breeze.

26
Soft-spoken words from her lips,
Sounded almost lyrical.
They helped disguise the cruelty of their intent.

27
I know this path,
I have travelled it well.
There is no option to pick the route less travelled,
And no opportunity to turn around.

28
I'm actively seeking out the glimmer in each day.
Recognize the triggers and lock them away.
Searching for the shines.
The joyful.
The sparkle.
The beauty.
The happy.

29

I promise to follow you,
But I don't promise to follow you through…
    forests of barbed wire and razor blades,
    swamps filled with alligators and snakes,
    or black meadows full of nightshade.

30

She held so many things in her hands,
her small hands,
and those things grew too heavy to hold.

July

1
Did you think I'd lie here happily,
tethered to your storm?

2
I swore at the stones that broke my bones,
but not the man who broke my soul.

3 *(Inspired by the Poets Have Something to Say podcast.)*
poets have something to say
with an arsenal of words
we work them like a puzzle
matching emotions to the phrases
beating within our heart

4 *(Independence Day)*
Fireworks bursting in air
As false patriots proudly wave
American flags manufactured in China
While "Born in the USA" blasts from
Sound systems of outlandishly large 4x4s
That belch out coal-black smoke
While immigrants are roughly handled
Accused of not being part of our original fabric
My heart grieves for a country
I was once proud of
But no longer recognize

5
It cannot be forced…writing.
Bulldozing through a…block.

6
I am caught between trying too hard,
and somehow not trying hard enough.

7
If no one wants me, that's ok,
There are days I don't want me.

8
I've been floating amongst the stars,
Untethered,
Hoping to catch hold of the moon.

9
There is no easy way to tell myself that I am,
And forever will be,
As average and dull as an old dirty gym sock.

10
bridges are built to close g a p s
however
words can do the same

11
How many poems did I write today?
Twelve.
Were any of them any good?
Nope.

12
We sit here,
Unashamed at the good trouble we caused,
And we look forward to marching ahead,
With bulldozers if necessary.

13
They want more words,
but I can't think past…
soul   death   love
breath   dark   void

14
Recycled words,
tumbled clean,
pristine and shiny.
Hung to dry in the early morning sun,
only for them to be covered in
green and yellow pollen by noon.

15
demented
endless
pain
pushed aside
wounds cleaned
not healed

scars
infected
ooze

16
The gravity of the situation is
that I've run out of words.
Without words
my emotions do not exist.

17
She marveled at the nearly invisible strands of silk
that were woven over the tops of blades of grass,
holding individual prisms of dew that caught the morning light.

18
You say quite confidently that you know what is in my head.

How could you?

I don't even know what is in there.
(Probably spiders and dust bunnies.)

19
I'm a fool.
Yes, I know I'm a fool,
a fool for loving you.

And I know,
you were foolish too.
Loving me for loving you.

20
seasons change
and so must we

21
You left the room,
leaving me wanting more.
        Your lips.
        Your eyes.
        Your hand on my thigh.

22
As the sun sets on another day,
I am reminded of how
My heart aches at the losses
I feel deeply within myself.
How we are on this earth with finite minutes
To live our lives as fully as possible.

23
What if I'm right,
but what if I'm wrong?
What's this crazy carousel I'm on?

You could be right,
but you could be wrong.
What's this crazy journey we're on?

24
Today feels like a strong voice day,
to be loud and confront things.

25
We stole the night,
and held the stars in our hands.

26
I will prepare a place for you,
but it will not be in my heart.

27
One of the worst parts of healing
is owning up to the hurt I caused myself.

28
Where do you go when you are sad and blue?
Do you visit the ghosts of you?

29
shrouded veil
death ascends

30
Aren't you tired of your heart feeling
h o l l o w?

31
Listen to the wind as she whispers your name.

August

1
Like the roots of an old oak,
writing keeps me grounded.

It holds me close to the reality
of this plane.

It reminds me of who I was,
and who I became.

2
You were right.
I don't want to be here anymore.

3
Love isn't always **loud**.

Sometimes it's as *soft* as a red cashmere sweater,
and as quiet as the falling snow.

4
You said…

I love you
hundreds of times.

But it always sounded like

You were placing

an order at a fast-food drive thru.

5 *(After days of dealing with brain fog.)*
There are days where
e x h a u s t i o n
interrupts my
t r a i n   o f   t h o u g h t,

and I feel *lost*
and *confused*

because   all   my   words
have   left   me.

6
trying
though you feel soul-tired
takes courage

7
will you be happy
when we are broken
b
r
o
k
e
n
like you?

8
will it ever dawn on you
that you could have been happy
by your own volition

9
She lay there, breathing in pain, swallowing blood and her pride.

Allowing herself to cough when she could no longer hold back.

She accepted that this could be the end, her final chapter.

Or as it so often is, a new season.

10
Walking through a maze of boxes…
his…
hers…
theirs…
Deciding if it's worth arguing over what they shared.

11
I grow impatient with the
cowards in charge
as they sit behind large expensive desks
pretending to be busy on their phone
refusing to fight.

12
"Spare me,"

She said between clenched teeth.

"I have no patience for silver-tied alibis."

13
empty vessels line up
one-by-one-by-one
glinting in the dusty sun

14
I am hunting for the gift receipt,
because I wouldn't consider your love a gift.

15 *(Thanks, Show Choir!)*
Blue Skies,
the melody haunting me
(thirty years later)
Nothing but blue skies do I see.

16 (Dementia sucks.)
Her memories and thoughts
come and go with the wind.

They glimmer like freshly fallen snowflakes
in the sunlight.

17
The lies we try to tell ourselves.
The shame we try to hide.
The truth we try to unbind.

18
Yes, I am writing to avoid housework.

19
One-by-one
the strands break
releasing the tethers
that held down her heart.

20
Secret black notebook
for secret feelings
    that one day I'll process.

But until then
I will ignore them
    as I shove the notebook under my bed.

21
She yearned for someone to
Breathe life into her again.
Her existence had become
Stagnant and stale.

22
She ran into the woods
tears raining from her face.
She knew the trees wouldn't judge her
for crying as her heart broke.

23
Mirror, mirror on the wall,
Why do you torture the self-confidence I'm trying to grow?

24
I feel a desperate need to write today
but all I've managed to write down was…

a grocery list full of snack foods I'm craving
&
a list for the liquor store to help me forget why I hurt.

25
She looked out the window as the world went past.
She longed for days that held meaning.

26
I am in need of a
·sunny deck
·cool gentle breeze
·pile of pillows
·couple of comfy blankets
·& a long nap after reading a book.

27 *(On my parents' anniversary.)*
they were once young
and very much in love
with the whole word ahead of them

28
I hope I remember
When once again I'm reborn
All the lessons I learned
The last time around

29

bumblebees
black and yellow sweater wearing
buzzingly happily
bumblebees

bumblebees
fuzzy wuzzy
bumblebee bottoms
sticking out of my flowers

30

walking away
questioning reality
scrutinizing details
letting go
brings peace

31

She wanted to be so many things,
She wished on so many stars,
But somehow…
She lost hold of all her dreams.

September

1
They spin a lovely fairy tale,
  and why shouldn't they?
Their lies don't hurt me,
  because I no longer care.
And I do enjoy a good story.

2
We are not responsible for things we could never control.
Even if it burns when we are held accountable.

3
Believe
I need to believe in me.
I need to read my own words
and believe.

4
So often
(during episodes of writer's block)
I will write whatever pops into my head
(even if it's rubbish)

Because two years from now I might read it
(work a little magic)
and give it life.

5
A glance at your past would break a hundred hearts.
You should have been loved.

6
I don't want to be the reason your ship sinks,
or why your vessel won't leave shore.

7
she strolled through the partially empty house
from room to room
slowly breathing in the
faded colors of a life she once knew

8
I write to process.
I write to heal.
I write to put things into perspective.

9
Blood-stained brick wall,
Head swirling in pain,
Too shocked to speak,
She sat watching him
Walking away, laughing.

10
She screamed for me to breathe,
but how can I breathe when someone
is holding my head below the water?

11
It will forever be a moment trapped in time.
Frozen in memory.

12
No matter how hard I tried,
I couldn't put your heart down.

13
when a soul meets September
when summer flowers no longer bloom

14
I remember being promised
a beautiful life
I'm almost certain I was

15
Would you shatter if you allowed yourself
to feel what's going on inside?
Would you break?
Dissolve?

16
He devoured her light,
the essence of her life.
Instead, he left her hollow
and cold.

17
There is a part of me
that is afraid to turn the page
in my own story.

18
you spotted me through the café window
you stopped and stared
you did not wave
nor did you throw a smile my way
you hung your head
and simply walked away

19 *(For the birthday boy.)*
One of the brightest stars in my sky
was born thirteen years ago today.

20
You start to develop a
sense for these things.

The unwanted?

Yes, for the unwanted.

21
I had not remembered how
HEAVY
his brown eyes could be.

22
Even if she had lived forever,

I would never have understood her,

And she would never have understood me.

23

Once upon a time, we all loved one another.
Now we sit, deleting all traces of each other's existence.

24

my brain is out of control,
pen in hand,
writing as fast as I can.

25

It has now been the seventh day of rain
under misery-grey skies
that have blocked the sun
from burning my midwest skin.

26

The woods are my sanctuary,
my personal church if you will.

I lack the words to describe
the peach they bring.

The quiet that soothes my heart,
or the healing it bestows.

27

I lie to myself.
Often.
It's unfortunate I believe me.

28
She gazed at the painting
hanging on the white wall.

She examined it closely
from several angles.

She wondered what the hell
she was looking at.

She wondered what the hell
the artist was trying to say.

She wondered why in the hell
she was crying.

29
two pens
one pencil
bit the dust
writing tonight

30
She thought she was honest with herself
about the situation she faced,
but the truth her heart told,
was exaggerated.

October

1 *(Inspired by Emilie Lindemann.)*
sitting cozy in a quiet nook
reading through stacks for inspiration
to extract all the hidden gold from within
old journals
torn notebooks
secret diaries
Post-It notes crinkled
dog-eared pages
highlighter marks faded
chiseling away with pen and pencil
then breathing life into memories
of wildflowers and all the trees

2
Summer holds strong
as autumn begins
to transform leaves
still clenching tight

3
When we forget to *exhale*
we slowly start to kill ourselves

4
summer
winding down
gusts blow
pulling at the leaves
starting to dry
brown and gold

5
what was done was final
she made up her mind
weeks ago
to strike the match
that would ignite an
upheaval of massive proportions

6
life turned her over
face-down into a muddy puddle
and said, "drink"

7
She decided that enough had happened in her life,
that made her thoroughly mad,
to stand up and yell,

"I'm sick of this shit!"

8
whispers can be deadly when done
in front of a very crowded room
when the one you are whispering with
has the volume control of a toddler

9
Autumn leaves
at their colorful peak.
Shimmering after a gentle rain
in dawn's light.

10

My words do not weave
an ambiguous cushion
for you to sit upon,
contemplating what
I am trying to say.

I am far too direct,
calling a spade a spade.

11

Breathing shallow and low
he's been restless for days.
Exhausted for years,
he tosses and turns.
Opening his eyes,
once in a while.
Trying to breathe deeper,
he closes his eyes again.
He longs for eternal sleep.

12

they spoke from both sides of their mouth
taking center stage whenever
there was an opportunity to entertain

to spin a tale of wonder
laced with spite and glee
knitting lies together
with arsenic and old lace

you could easily see the joy
flame within their face

13

I'm tired of fighting a war with myself,
because I know I can never win.

14

He said...
    The Devil might just get me yet.
I laughed because...
    He didn't know that is exactly who I was.

15

I spied the Grey Witch the other day
sitting up in the old-gnarled tree
at the Maple Wood Cemetery.

She recognized me,
from all those years past,
when I found her missing toad.

She nodded her head,
while wrinkling her nose,
and a package dropped at my feet

I picked it up,
with surprise and glee,
and found inside black salt, quartz, and honey.

I smiled and waved,
she nodded again,
and in a blink, she had flown away.

16
I am comfortable with death.
Correction: I am comfortable with my own death.

17 *(For KLC)*
she was a healer,
a feeler,
a seer,
a candle that could not be dimmed.

18
signs and flags proudly waving
car horns blaring
people cheering
there are no Kings today

19
the nightmares we cling to...
the ones that haunt the halls...
they twist and slither...
all along the walls

they scream and wail...
until you wake...
but you can't see them...
with eyes open

20
a tornado of leaves
tried to whisk me away

21
Have you ever noticed
how quiet the Devil's
footsteps are?

22
the dreams escaped her lips
rolled out into the ether
swirled around his head
until he fell into a slumber
deep and somber
he saw and felt everything
she had seen and experienced
in her very short life

23 *(To my sister on her birthday.)*
The laughter always outweighed the hair pulling.
Like when we went on vacation to "The Big Dirt,"
or we put on fresh socks before bed while camping,
and when Pamela was doing something crazy.
The way we would drive people crazy,
if there were strawberry milkshakes after football.
The best part is that no one knows what any of this means,
except you and me.

24 *(For JMB)*
She is a child of the forest
untamed and free
her hair tangled by the breeze

25
she wrote a name on paper
three times for luck

folded and wrapped it around an anointed black candle
bound it together with twine

held the packet close to her chest
she whispered a spell in a low hush
and lit that candle ablaze while she held tight

she let that candle wax drip onto a silver tray
then she planted the candle in the black puddle

she chanted and hummed the name softly
three times for luck
and buried that name with smoke and ash

26
the night we spoke to the dead...
under the full blood moon...
a chill in the air...
beasties stirring in the twilight...
candles flitting on the dank grass...

the night they answered back...
has left me shivering...
as if someone walked across my grave...
cursing me from that moment...
until eternity...

27
she waits at the crossroads that bleed
poor ol' Annabelle Lee
no one knows who she waits on
or who her heart longs for
but she has stood there for years
at the crossroads that bleed
poor ol' Annabelle Lee

28
There is something special about the night air in October.
The crickets trilling,
the toads croaking,
the owls hooting,
and the breeze carrying the scent of dried pine needles and leaves.

29
My heart was heavy,
My soul felt cold,
Concerning the way the world,
Disposed of those they felt were...lesser than.
Yet they claimed to know God.

30
Please consider Wisdom's feelings.
Especially when you hear her...
E X A S P E R A T E D *sighs*
when you've done something...silly
after you ignored her advice.

31
illuminated under the
full moon of Halloween

stand thirteen stones
arranged in a perfect circle

each stone bears a name
that is older than time

as the stones begin to sing
the old gods start to stir

the veil begins to thin
allowing the ancestors to step through

November

1
what more can one say, or do
as the maple trees shed their final leaves
and the grey skies of winter settle in

2
The four of us are sitting in a cafe,
the table next to an old brick wall
that features a mural of a deer.

Far away from the comforts of home,
we chatted over strong coffee,
a cinnamon roll,
and an order of hashbrowns.

We laughed over old stories,
and even older memories,
feeling the depths of someone missing.

3
if you leave him this way
by the side of the road
dust from your truck
blowing into his eyes
as you stick out your hand
waving goodbye
you'll forever be haunted
by his cries

4
It's easy to break when you are
held together by sand and brittle autumn leaves.

5
I wouldn't have taken notice of you
Among the rust and brown leaves
But you flicked your white tail
As you enjoyed the late autumn apples
That fell to the damp grass
With an echo and a thud.

6
She wore her birthday crown and a smile on her face,
while she sat in her wheelchair, in an unfamiliar place.

She studied every face that walked by,
some she remembered, but many were simply "strangers".

She spun us tall tales while being a little sassy,
and we laughed as we soaked up each word, with a shake of our heads.

We were trying to remember each moment, over store-bought cake and cookies, making our own birthday wishes that things weren't quite like this.

7
The autumn of her life had just begun.
It was the season of letting go of everything
she had been carrying for the last two seasons.

She did this in her backyard,
as the leaves swirled around
and danced with her in relief.

8
There is an ache
I cannot ignore
That longs to heal you

9
you painted me in gold and greens
on a large black canvas
daubing in the deepest purple clouds
I had ever seen
and you drew a moon of silver in the corner
and a million stars that shone

10
she strikes a match
throws it onto the dry wood
neatly stacked in the fireplace

the fire blazes upwards
it crackles and says her name
fire always remembers a face

11
When you held my hand
I thought I knew.
But I was clearly mistaken,
because I knew nothing.

12
She should have buried herself with her own words.

13
and...
just like that...
you've pushed me...
to the point where I...
no longer care...

14
Smoke and ash whispers
float on the night breeze
from the hollow of an old tree.

The tree whispers your secrets
so you can be free
no longer held down by burdensome memories

15
Autumn is giving us one last taste of summer.
I'll embrace it like a day at the lake.

Barefoot,
hair flowing down my back in waves tangled by the breeze.

Sunlight bouncing off the last of the colorful leaves.

I'm storing the warm sun in canning jars,
to open on bitter cold winter mornings.

16
His words stripped away at my soul.
My words healed it.

17
You look at me,
eyes wide,
with impatient ears.

I do not know what answer,
you long to hear.

18
Do you feel these words as I feel them, as you read them?

Can you taste the bitter and the sweet, as I speak them?

Are you struggling to breathe them in, and exhale their meaning?

Words are alive!

19
If she could have everything she longed for,
all her heart's desire,
she would still feel empty and hollow,
because she refuses to remove the rusted colander,
that has replaced her heart.

20
the silence I felt between us
was not born of emptiness,
but of our souls withering
from not being fed.

21
It wasn't the goodbye that wrecked me,
it was the way you smiled when you first said, "hello".

22
It is unnerving to be seen
once you've unveiled yourself.
It is difficult to wrap yourself up again.

23
in the end
we become the dust
that settles onto
some strangers
coffee table

24
There are words I have never dared to speak.
I could barely think them...
let alone breathe them.

25
She never thought that once,
maybe once,
it would be ok to save herself first.

26
If I were to meet you in another lifetime,
I would run in the opposite direction.

27 *(Thanksgiving Day)*
There have been times when I might not have been as gracious as I should be.

In times of darkness, it's not always easy to spot the light beaming on the horizon.

However, I have learned during those times that I have very little control over what happens, but I can control how I respond.

There is no use fighting with the wind.

I am truly grateful for every lesson I have learned and each blessing I have received.

28
November rains soon turned to slush,
that grew dirty under giant lifted trucks.

29
I watched you walk away
knowing that I could never save you,
and knowing you would never be strong enough
to save yourself.

30
my heart in turmoil
over what is right
and what should stay silent
buried inside it's own chamber

December

1
When no one is there,
and the night seems endless and cold.
When you can't sleep,
but still find the energy to cry.
When you contemplate your purpose,
yet somehow lost your beliefs.
When you feel all hope has died,
the sun rises.

2
The mountains and ocean are calling me to warmer temps.
My soul needs to thaw.

3 *(My favorite walks.)*
winter night
full moon
clear sky
stars shining
cold crisp air
train whistle blows
from beyond the silence

4
I have woven splinters of time
together with threads of silver and gold.
Each time I reach for another fragment
my fingers tingle from the
precious moments
trapped within.

5
Listen to the wind
as she calls your name.

6
I try not to remember how alone I feel sometimes.

I push the feelings aside,
as if I was sweeping the kitchen floor or dusting the living room.

I try not to remember how alone I feel sometimes.

I try to push those feelings down,
in the same way I try to push more garbage into an already full bag.

7
Feeling as if she had no choice,
she started running towards the edge of the world.
Ignoring everything her conscience screamed at her,
and every memory that clung to her soul.

8
you stole from me
you stole my light
my joy
my innocence
you took away a sacred piece of me
that you could never give back

9

The burden sat heavy in the middle of her chest,
not allowing her to breathe.

10

When you reach out into the void,
searching for something,
not knowing what it is you seek,
your heart often falls in love with something,
or someone,
you really don't need.

11

Cold coffee sits muddy in my mug,
it brings no warmth.
Misty grey-filled skies,
longing to let go.

Gods, why can't I?

12

Give me something to believe in.
Put a song in my heart to sing.
Let the world recognize
that we are the change we need.

13

Ancestral threads bind our souls through generations.
Sometimes those threads tangle and develop knots.

14
She says she doesn't remember,
but she lies to save what little bit of innocence she has left,
because...
            she remembers
                                    E V E R Y T H I N G.

15
you are a breaker of people
the hoarder of souls

you crush what little is left
from what once made them whole

16
She reminded me of a glass,
full of lemonade and bobbing ice cubes.

The ice cubes fighting each other
to rise to the top of the glass,
only to find out that you melt first.

17
It's been a long time coming.

We ignored the writing
that was on the wall,
in bold black letters,
warning us to resist.

To run.

18
she runs outside into the night air
far away from the comforts of her home

        she trips
        falling in the knee-deep snow

crying towards the stars
not from the cold

        but from all the souls
        that surround her own

her frozen tears
don't slide down her face

        but they glitter in the moonlight
        as her heart breaks

19
Out of the corner of my eye,
I saw the shadow as it reached for me.
I turned around so quickly,
I frightened it away.

20
You ambushed me in a haze of cigarette smoke and strong cologne. Singing melodies, out of tune, that no one listens to anymore.

Preaching about the ridiculous notions of budding romance between men and women.

21
I sit here in the flicker of the mid-winter candle glow,
holding the book of my life in my lap.

The chapter titled...Regrets...begins with the line...

She regrets few things about her life.
However, the thing she absolutely regrets is not loving herself.

22
Long, lonely day of winter...
no sun to warm my face.

Only the grey cloak of cold...
unforgiving winds.

23
The stars appeared
In the old winter sky
Breathless and blushing
They twinkled in anticipation
Waiting for the meteors to smolder across the sky

24
the beautiful peace found on Christmas Eve

soft glow of candles

and illuminated tree

chorus of angels sing as children doze off to sleep

25
There is a certain magic
in the stillness found
on Christmas morning.

The snow gently falling
crisp and clean
coating the evergreens.

The lights from the yuletide tree
offers a warm glow
while candles flicker nearby.

The quiet offers me time to reflect
on all the good in the world
that is sometimes difficult to see.

But my thoughts are soon interrupted
by joyful noises
bounding down the stairs.

26
curious, dark-eyed sullen child
wearing a ripped coat two sizes too small
and shoes with holes
empty tummy and heavy heart
begging without saying a word

I swear I can feel the pieces of your heart
scatter in the north winds
as you contemplate what your place in the world is
when strangers pass you on the sidewalk
without giving you a glance

27
She always fancied herself as Alice in Wonderland,
but in reality,
she was only ever finding herself falling down rabbit holes
while using Google.

28
The blue sky was barren.
The wind bitter,
biting noses that peeked out from behind scarves.
Speckling our eyelashes in frosty crystals.
Though the sun shone,
we felt no warmth.

29
Once the caterpillar finally found the warmth
and comfort of a cocoon,
she vowed to never leave the one place
she finally felt safe.

30
Time is the worst illusion of all.
"There is always tomorrow."

But is there?
We are not promised time to mend fences, say our piece,
or tell those we love that we do love them.

Time disappears as quickly as we draw breath,
or blink.

31

The dawn of a new year,
is on the horizon.

Bringing with it,
all the hopes and possibilities
that last year forgot to bring.

Acknowledgements

I would like to take this moment to thank my family and friends for not only buying my books, but asking me about my current projects, and listening with very patient ears as I drone on about my ideas. For some of you, I know my writing is not easy to digest, and yet here you are, loving me as I am. I cannot put into words how much that means to me.

The following people helped me not only polish the book you hold in your hands, but they were my sounding board, the questioners, the first readers, the ones who held me accountable and kept me to task. JoAnna Burditt, Kelli Cornelius, Henry Hinojos, and Scott Hinojos, maybe one day I can start paying you, because you have certainly earned it. Thank you for always being there and being patient with me. I honestly cannot imagine doing this without you.

To those who have purchased my books, I'm still flabbergasted but eternally grateful that you believe in me enough to spend money on words I put down on some paper. I will always be amazed by that.

About the Author

Stacy Hinojos is an avid writer of poetry and short stories.
When she isn't writing and drinking coffee,
she's reading and drinking coffee.

She resides in Central Wisconsin with her husband and their son.

Coffee-Stained Reflections is Stacy's fourth book.

Find more of their work:
https://www.thesewords.blog/

Other Works by Stacy Hinojos

These Words
A Thousand Melodies
Everything but a Novel

available at Amazon.com and BookShop.org

www.ingramcontent.com/pod-product-compliance
Lightning Source LLC
LaVergne TN
LVHW010935110826
845149LV00013B/2613

* 9 7 9 8 9 9 1 2 8 0 7 3 0 *